NFL RIVALRIES

BEARS VS. PACKERS

By Anthony K. Hewson

Kaleidoscope
Minneapolis, MN

Your Front Row Seat to the Games

This edition first published in 2020 by Kaleidoscope Publishing, Inc.

For information regarding permission, write to
Kaleidoscope Publishing, Inc.
6012 Blue Circle Drive
Minnetonka, MN 55343

Library of Congress Control Number
2019939141

ISBN
978-1-64519-079-0 (library bound)
978-1-64494-164-5 (paperback)
978-1-64519-180-3 (ebook)

Printed in the United States of America.

TABLE OF CONTENTS

CHAPTER 1

For the Crown

The Green Bay Packers and Chicago Bears play every year. They have since 1921. But something was different on January 23, 2011. A trip to the Super Bowl was on the line.

It was cold in Chicago. But that did not stop Bears fans. More than 62,000 came out to Soldier Field. They filled the stadium. The fans cheered loudly.

PLAYOFF HISTORY

The 2011 game was the second playoff meeting between the teams. The first one came in 1941. The Bears won 33–14.

It was a cold day, but the sun shone brightly as the Bears faced the Packers.

The players could see their breath. The cold made it hard to play. Neither team could move the ball much. But Green Bay did better. It was 14–0 Packers at halftime.

FUN FACT
The Packers won ten games in the 2010–2011 season. The Bears won eleven.

Caleb Hanie, left, helped the Bears score more points and make it a close game.

The Bears' starting quarterback was Jay Cutler. He hurt his knee. He had to leave the game. The **backup** quarterback was Todd Collins. He did not play well. Backup Caleb Hanie came in. He played better. The Bears made it close. They came within seven points.

They had one last chance to tie. Hanie led them down the field. They got to Green Bay's 29-yard line. There were 47 seconds left. It was fourth down.

Hanie took the **snap**. Defenders rushed at him. He looked over the field. He threw to receiver Johnny Knox. But Knox was covered. Green Bay's Sam Shields ran to the ball. He got in front of Knox. Shields **intercepted** the pass. The Bears' chance to win vanished. The Packers won 21–14.

The Bears then watched their rival play in the Super Bowl. To make it worse, the Packers won. It was another chapter in a classic NFL rivalry.

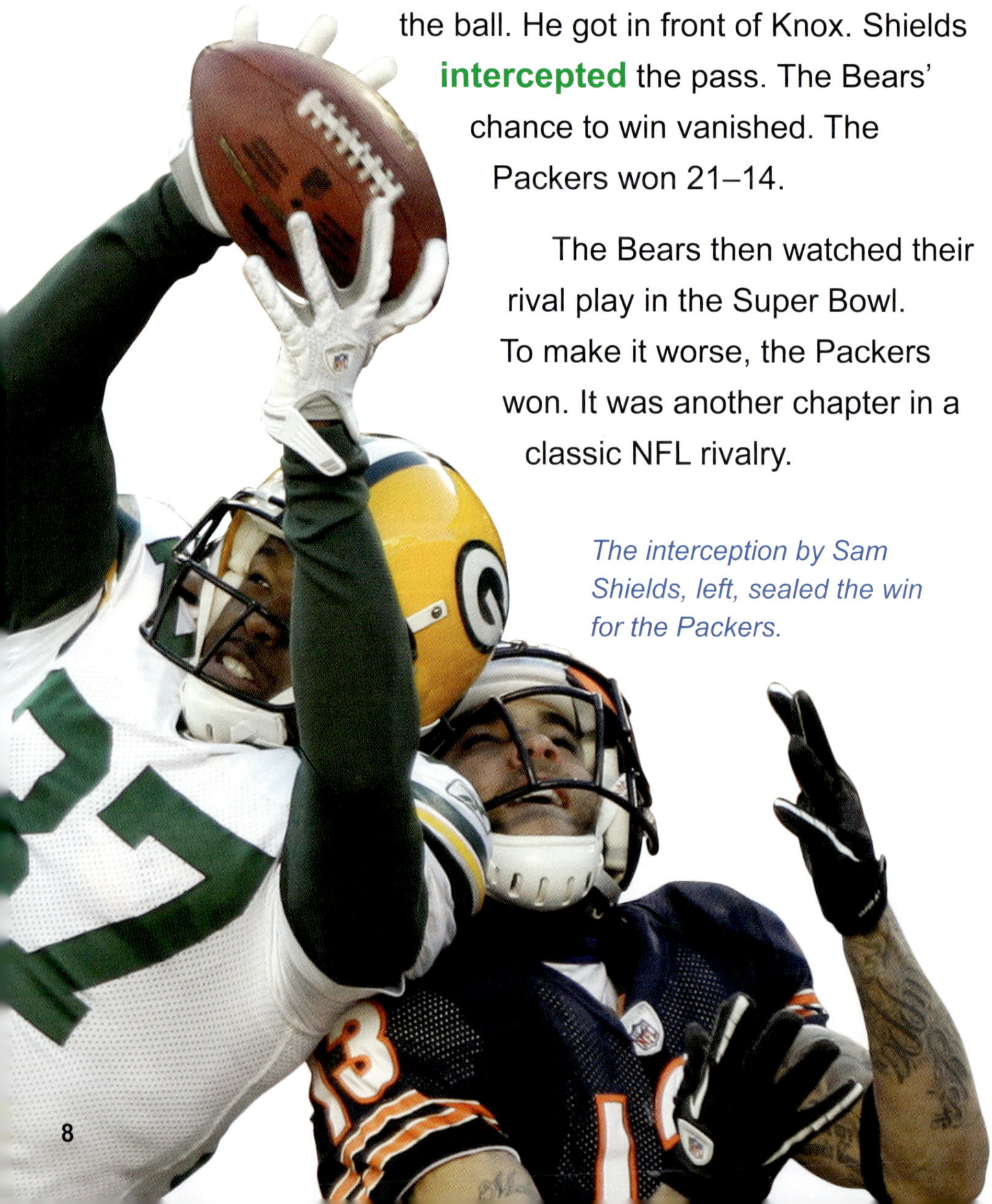

The interception by Sam Shields, left, sealed the win for the Packers.

HEAD TO HEAD

STATS

Through the 2018 season

CHICAGO		GREEN BAY
95	WINS	97
49.5	WINNING PERCENTAGE	50.5
3,361	POINTS SCORED	3,399
1	PLAYOFF WINS	1
8 (1985–88)	LONGEST WIN STREAK	(1994–98) 10
1	TOTAL SUPER BOWL VICTORIES	4

CHAPTER 2

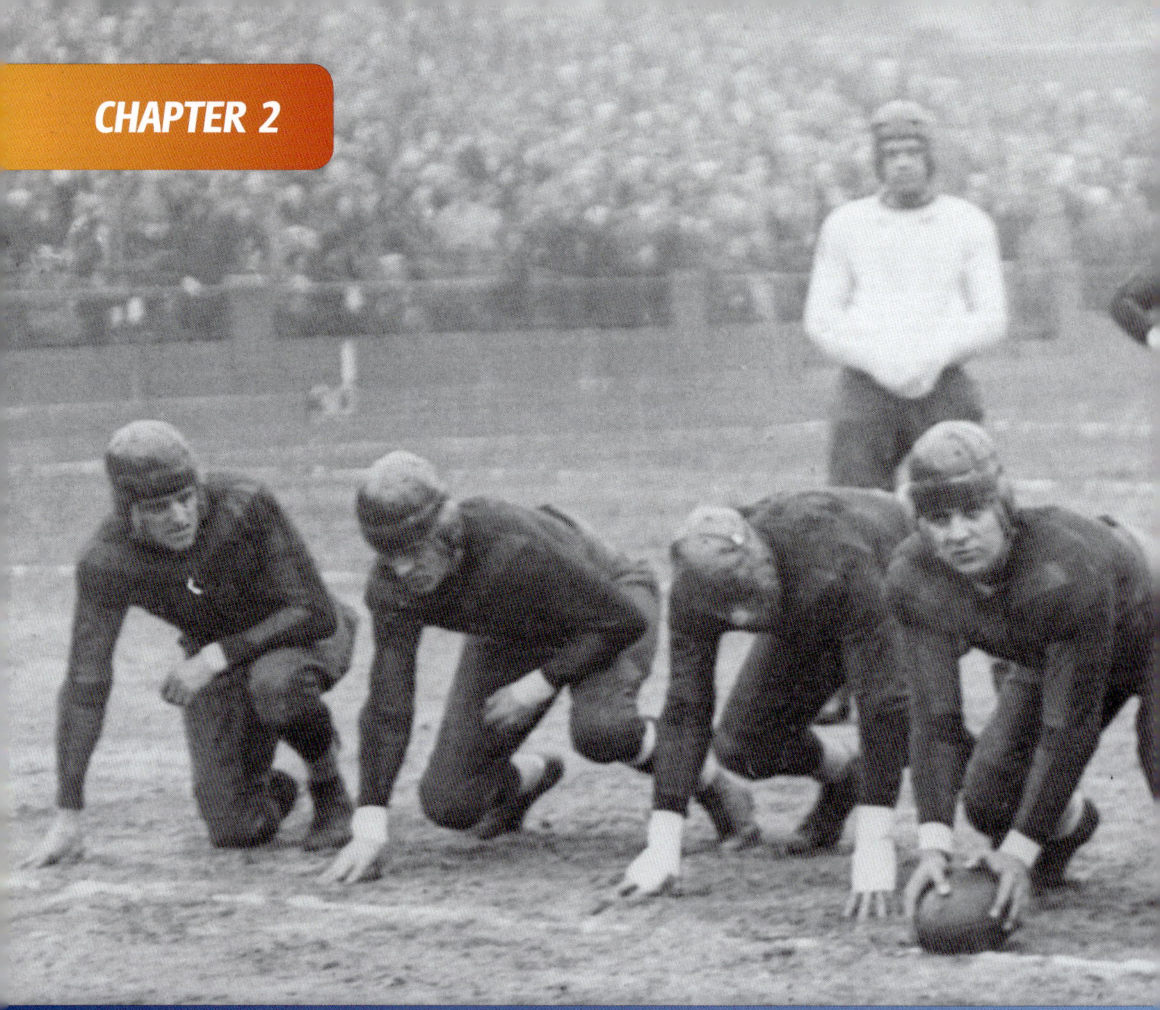

The Most-Played Rivalry

Pete Stinchcomb touched the frozen Chicago ground. It was November 27, 1921. The Bears and Packers were meeting for the first time. At that time the Bears were called the Staleys. And the teams were not yet rivals.

Stinchcomb was a Staleys running back. He scored the first touchdown that day. He ran the ball 45 yards.

Football uniforms in the 1920s looked very different from how they look today.

He avoided tackles. The crowd of 7,000 roared in delight. Chicago won 20–0. They were named the Bears the next year. A rivalry had begun.

Usually the Bears came out on top. They won six titles from 1932 to 1946. One of those came in 1941. They had to beat Green Bay to earn it.

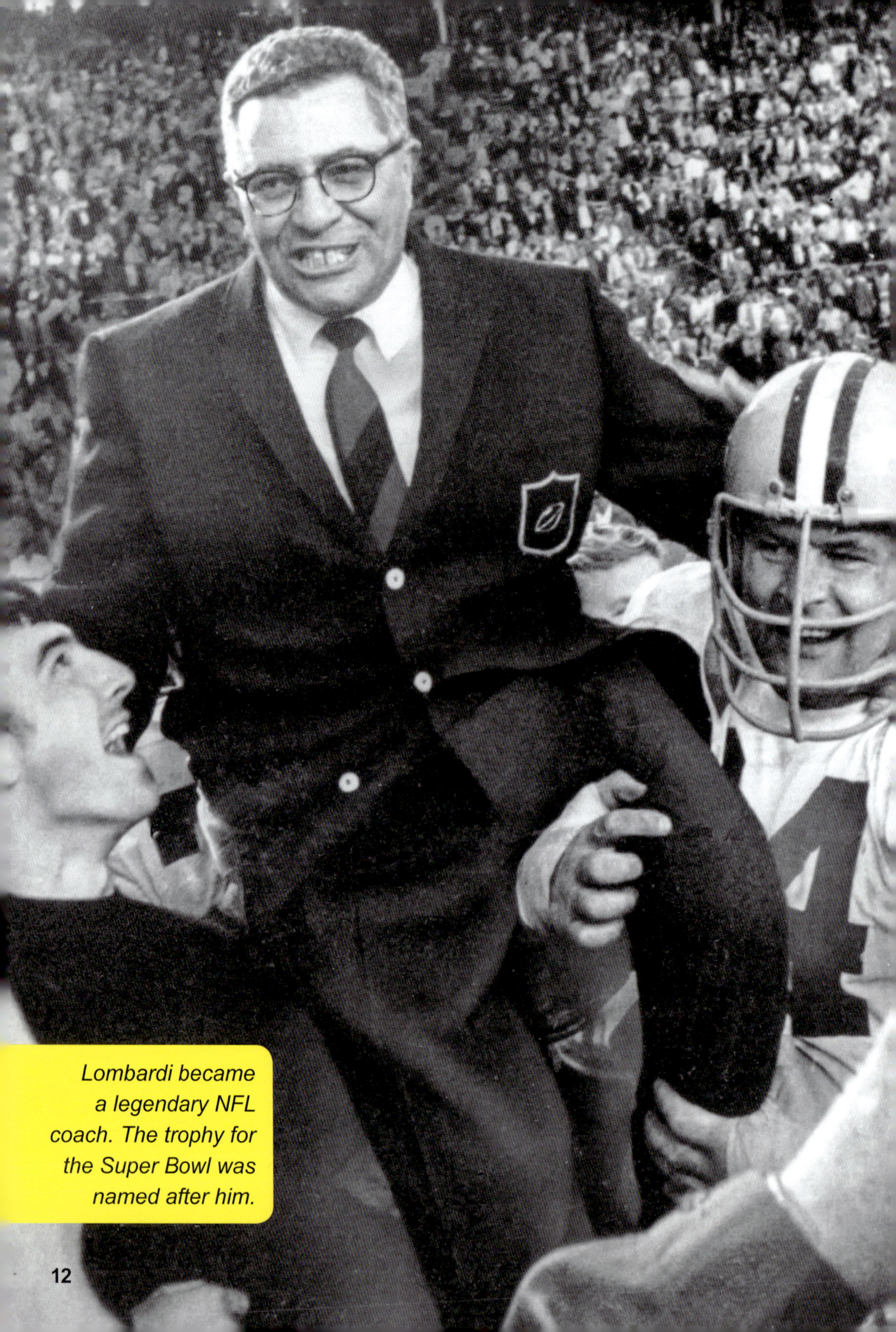

Lombardi became a legendary NFL coach. The trophy for the Super Bowl was named after him.

The game was in Chicago. More than 43,000 fans packed the stands. It was in December and cold again. Disaster struck the Bears early. They fumbled the kickoff. The ball bounced along the field. It tumbled to Green Bay.

The Packers scored a 1-yard touchdown. But the Bears answered. Hugh Gallarneau fielded a **punt**. He tore up the field. He left every Packer in the dust. It was an 81-yard touchdown. The Bears went on to win 33–14.

Green Bay hired Vince Lombardi as coach in 1959. Lombardi turned the Packers into winners. They started to beat the Bears a lot more. The 1962 Packers went 13–1. The Bears were helpless that year. They lost to the Packers 49–0. Jim Taylor ran all over Chicago. He had three touchdowns and 126 yards. It was the Bears' worst loss in the rivalry. They lost again later that year. The Bears spent all **offseason** working on a plan to beat Green Bay. The plan worked. They won both games in 1963.

FUN FACT
Lombardi won 105 games in his coaching career. He lost just thirty-five.

The Bears had a great defense in the 1980s. They beat Green Bay 61–7 on December 7, 1980. But the Bears still weren't happy. "We wanted 100 points," said Bears defensive end Dan Hampton. The rivalry was as heated as ever.

The 1990s and 2000s were about quarterbacks. The Packers had two stars in a row. First came Brett Favre. Then Aaron Rodgers took over. Both passers were great against the Bears. Green Bay took the all-time series lead in 2017. The Bears had work to do to come back.

The 1985 Bears had a fantastic defense. They won the Super Bowl in January 1986.

THE ACCIDENTAL TOUCHDOWN

In a September 1980 game, the Packers struggled to score a touchdown. They finally got one by accident. They lined up for a field goal. The kicker, Chester Marcol, got his foot on the ball. It flew into the air. But then the kick was blocked by a Bears defender. The ball bounced right back into Marcol's hands. He ran around the left side for a surprising touchdown.

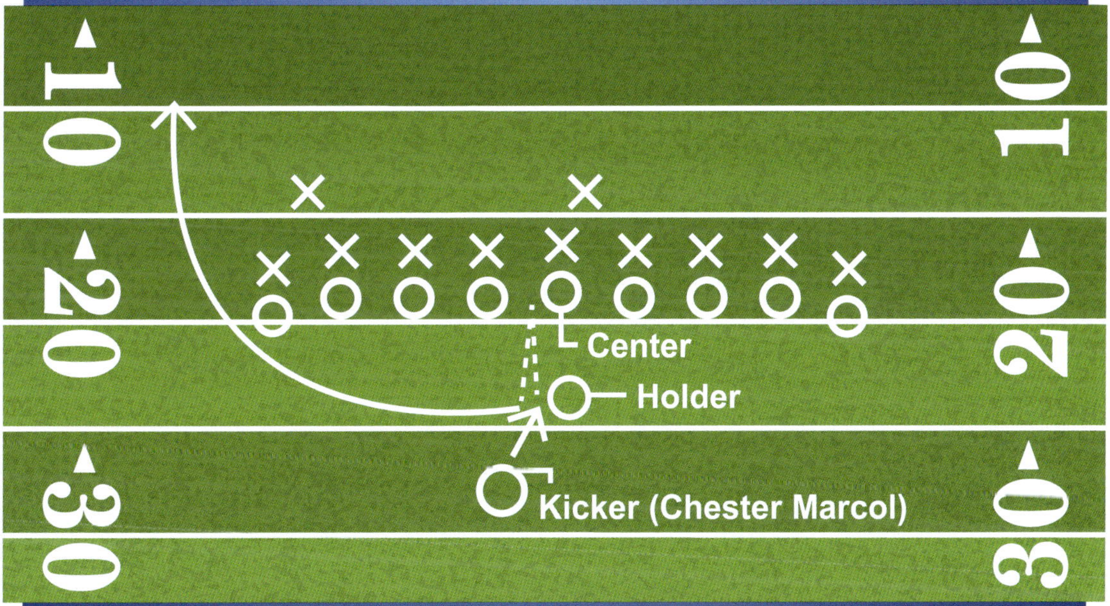

CHAPTER 3

Legendary Players

The Bears had the advantage. It was Monday Night Football at Soldier Field. The date was September 11, 1995. Green Bay was on its own 1-yard line.

But the Packers had Brett Favre. If anyone could get out of this mess, it was him. He was one of the best in the NFL. And he shined against the Bears. Bears fans always hated facing him.

Favre faced third down and 10. Bears fans were screaming at him. He took the snap. The Bears rushed at him. But Favre did not panic. He faked a throw. A defender was inches away. Then Favre threw for real. It was just in time. He found Robert Brooks running alone. The play went for a 99-yard touchdown.

Soldier Field in Chicago

Favre was one of the most talented quarterbacks ever.

Favre later left the Packers. But things did not get easier for the Bears. Aaron Rodgers was just as good. And he was great against the Bears. Through 2018, he had a 16–5 record against them.

FUN FACT
In 2018, Rodgers threw 402 straight passes without an interception.

Mack's speed and power make him a tough opponent on the football field.

The Bears and Packers played to open the 2018 season. Chicago had just signed Khalil Mack. He was a talented defender. People expected the Bears to improve.

Mack had a huge game. He forced two **turnovers**. Chicago built a lead. They were winning 20–0 at halftime. But Rodgers had more magic. He led Green Bay back to within six points. Could the Bears hold on?

By 2018, Cobb had been a top Packers receiver for many years.

FUN FACT
The Bears and Packers have sixty-five Hall of Famers.

Green Bay faced third and 10. The clock showed 2:28 to go. Rodgers dropped back. Mack rushed toward him. But then Rodgers started to pass. Mack tried to go cover a receiver. It was too late. The ball soared through the air. Randall Cobb grabbed it. He took off. Bears players raced after him. But they could not catch Cobb. He ran the ball 75 yards for the score. The Packers won.

Mack and the Bears had the last laugh in 2018. They beat the Packers in December. This knocked the Packers out of the playoffs. Mack continued the tradition of strong Bears defenders. The rivalry has included many more great players. All of them have played in rivalry games.

Lambeau Field in Green Bay

SWEETNESS

Bears running back Walter Payton is one of the best NFL players ever. His nickname was Sweetness. He had a great career against Green Bay. One game in 1977 was amazing. He rushed for 205 yards and two touchdowns.

CHAPTER 4

Serious Business

Lovie Smith stepped to the microphone. It was January 15, 2004. He was the new Bears coach. Smith had just been hired. He was speaking to reporters for the first time.

The Bears had a long history. They had many traditions. Smith knew the rivalry was important. He talked about the team's goals. "The number one goal is to beat Green Bay," he said.

Lovie Smith understood how important the Bears' rivalry with the Packers is.

Green Bay Packers fans of all ages are passionate about their team.

The players take the rivalry seriously. So do the fans. Russell Beckman is a Packers fan. In 2016, he had tickets to their game in Chicago. He had the chance to visit the sideline. But the Bears told him no. He could not wear Packers gear there.

Wisconsin and Illinois border each other. Sometimes, the rivalry divides a family. Fans in a family choose different teams. This makes the rivalry even more personal.

Rivalry Map

N
W
E
S
Minnesota
Green Bay Packers
Lambeau Field
Green Bay, Wisconsin
Michigan
Iowa
Chicago Bears
Soldier Field
Chicago, Illinois
Ohio
Indiana
Missouri
Kentucky

The Kaufmann family is from Woodstock, Illinois. Dad Jeff is from Illinois. Mom Tara is from Wisconsin. Some of their kids are Packers fans. Others are Bears fans. One year, Tara's parents wanted to get Packers gear for the kids. The Bears fans were not pleased. "I would have burned it," said eleven-year-old Isaac.

Fans keep the rivalry alive. They pass it on to the next generation. That's why the Packers–Bears rivalry is one of the NFL's best.

FUN FACT

Wisconsin is known for its cheese. Packers fans sometimes wear cheese-shaped hats.

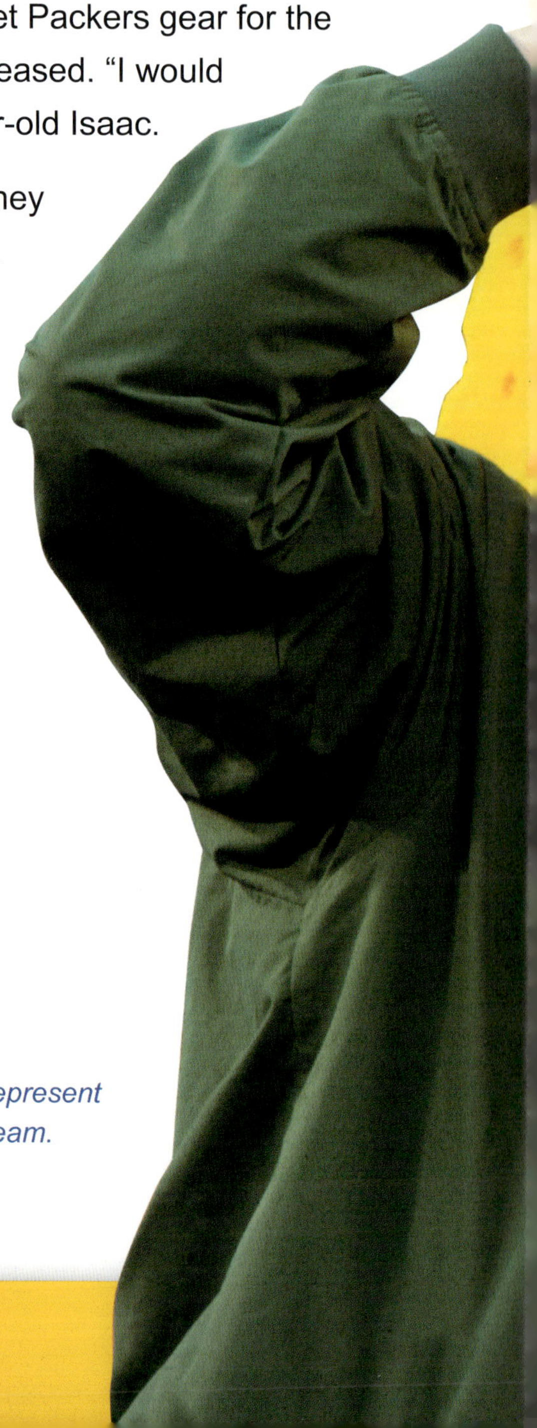

Fans love to represent their favorite team.

BEYOND THE BOOK

After reading the book, it's time to think about what you learned. Try the following exercises to jumpstart your ideas.

THINK

THAT'S NEWS TO ME. Chapter One talks about Aaron Rodgers' career against the Bears. What kinds of news sources could you use to learn more about this? What kind of information might you get from those sources?

CREATE

SHARPEN YOUR RESEARCH SKILLS. Chapter Two talks about the stars that have played for both the Bears and Packers. Where would you go to find more information about those players? Write a paragraph outlining a research plan to find out more.

SHARE

WHAT'S YOUR OPINION? Chapter Two says that the Bears and Packers became rivals. Using facts and evidence you learned in the text, how would you support this opinion? How might you disagree with it? Share your position with a friend. Were they convinced by your position?

GROW

REAL-LIFE RESEARCH. It is one thing to read about a topic. But a lot can be learned from actually experiencing the topic in person. Where would you go to learn more about the Bears-Packers rivalry? What other things could you learn there?

RESEARCH NINJA

Visit www.ninjaresearcher.com/0790 to learn how to take your research skills and book report writing to the next level!

RESEARCH

DIGITAL LITERACY TOOLS

SEARCH LIKE A PRO

Learn about how to use search engines to find useful websites.

FACT OR FAKE?

Discover how you can tell a trusted website from an untrustworthy resource.

TEXT DETECTIVE

Explore how to zero in on the information you need most.

SHOW YOUR WORK

Research responsibly—learn how to cite sources.

WRITE

GET TO THE POINT

Learn how to express your main ideas.

PLAN OF ATTACK

Learn prewriting exercises and create an outline.

DOWNLOADABLE REPORT FORMS

Further Resources

BOOKS

Osborne, M. K. *Superstars of the Chicago Bears*. Amicus, 2019.

Osborne, M. K. *Superstars of the Green Bay Packers*. Amicus, 2019.

Wilner, Barry. *NFL's Top Ten Rivalries*. Abdo Publishing, 2018.

WEBSITES

FACTSURFER

Factsurfer.com gives you a safe, fun way to find more information.

1. Go to www.factsurfer.com.
2. Enter "Bears vs. Packers" into the search box and click 🔍.
3. Select your book cover to see a list of related websites.

Glossary

backup: A backup is a second option when the first option is not available. The backup came in to play instead of the starter.

intercepted: A ball is intercepted when a defensive player catches it instead of the intended receiver. Sam Shields intercepted Caleb Hanie's pass.

offseason: The offseason is the time between seasons when no teams are playing. The player used the offseason to heal from injury.

playoff: A playoff is a tournament held after the season to determine a champion. The Packers made a playoff appearance after the 2010 season.

punt: A punt is when a team with the ball kicks it to the other team to change possession. The Bears decided to punt on fourth down.

snap: The center snaps the ball to the quarterback to start the play. Bears quarterback Jay Cutler took the snap.

turnovers: Turnovers are lost fumbles or interceptions. The Bears committed two turnovers against the Packers.

Index

PHOTO CREDITS

The images in this book are reproduced through the courtesy of: Jeff Haynes/Panini/AP Images, front cover (left); Kevin Terrell/AP Images, front cover (right); EFKS/Shutterstock Images, front cover (field); Jeff Bukowski/Shutterstock Images, pp. 3 (left), 3 (right); David Stluka/AP Images, pp. 4–5, 17; Tom Hauck/AP Images, pp. 6–7; David J. Phillip/AP Images, p. 8; Red Line Editorial, pp. 9, 25; Bettmann/Getty Images, pp. 10–11; AP Images, p. 12; Mtsaride/Shutterstock Images, p. 13; Paul Spinelli/AP Images, p. 14; enterlinedesign/Shutterstock Images, p. 15; Richard Cavalleri/Shutterstock Images, p. 16; Scott Boehm/AP Images, pp. 18–19, 30; Morry Gash/AP Images, p. 20; timhughes/iStockphoto, p. 21; Max Herman/Shutterstock Images, p. 22; Tom DiPace/AP Images, pp. 22–23; James.Pintar/Shutterstock Images, p. 24; Kiichiro Sato/AP Images, pp. 26–27.

ABOUT THE AUTHOR

Anthony K. Hewson is a children's book author originally from San Diego. After a long career in aviation, he and his wife retired to San Rafael, California, where they enjoy spending time with their dogs and grandchildren.